*All children have
a great ambition to read
to themselves...*

*and a sense of achievement when they can do so.
The* **read it yourself** *series has been devised to
satisfy their ambition. Since many children learn
from the Ladybird Key Words Reading Scheme,
these stories have been based to a large extent
on the Key Words List, and the tales chosen are
those with which children are likely to be familiar.*

*The series can of course be used as
supplementary reading for any reading scheme.*
Hansel and Gretel *is intended for children reading
up to Book 2c of the Ladybird Reading Scheme.
The following words are additional to the
vocabulary used at that level —*

Hansel, Gretel, father, woodcutter,
stepmother, food, sleep, gets, up,
pebbles, morning, out, wood, drops,
as, lights, fire, stay, gone, good,
can't, breadcrumbs, house, eat,
witch, puts, cage, hot, treasure,
find, way

*A list of other titles at the same level will be
found on the back cover.*

Hansel and Gretel

by Fran Hunia
illustrated by Anna Dzierzek

Ladybird Books Loughborough

Here are
Hansel and Gretel.

Here is
Hansel and Gretel's
father,
the woodcutter.

This is
Hansel and Gretel's
stepmother.

The stepmother says
to the woodcutter,
We have no food.
Hansel and Gretel
have to go.

No, says the
woodcutter.

The stepmother says,
Yes. They have to go.

The woodcutter
and the stepmother
go to sleep.

Hansel gets up.

He looks
for some pebbles.

In the morning
the stepmother says,
Get up, Hansel.
Get up, Gretel.
We have to go out
to get some wood.

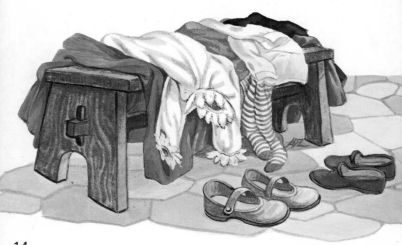

They go
into the woods.
Hansel drops
the pebbles
as they go.

The woodcutter
lights a fire.

You stay here,
Hansel and Gretel,
he says.
We are going to look
for some wood.

Hansel and Gretel
go to sleep.

The woodcutter
and the stepmother
go home.

The fire
has gone out.

Hansel and Gretel
get up.

They look
for the pebbles.

Look, says Hansel.
Here are the pebbles.
We can go home.

Hansel and Gretel
go home.

The woodcutter
jumps up.
Hansel and Gretel!
he says.
It is good
to have you home.

The woodcutter says
to the stepmother,
I want Hansel
and Gretel to stay
here.

No, says
the stepmother.
We have no food.
Hansel and Gretel
have to go.

The woodcutter and
the stepmother
go to sleep.

Hansel gets up
to look
for some pebbles.

He can't get out.

In the morning
the stepmother says,
Get up, Hansel.
Get up, Gretel.
We have to go out
to get some wood.

They go
into the woods.

Hansel has
no pebbles.

He drops
some breadcrumbs.

The woodcutter
lights a fire.
Stay here,
Hansel and Gretel,
he says. We are going
to get some wood.

Hansel and Gretel,
go to sleep.
The woodcutter
and the stepmother
go home.

The fire is out.

Hansel and Gretel
get up.

They want to go home.

They look
for the breadcrumbs.

The breadcrumbs
have gone.

Hansel and Gretel
can't go home.

Hansel and Gretel
come to a house.

Gretel says,
this house is good
to eat.

They eat and eat.

38

A witch comes out.
You can come in,
says the witch.

The witch wants to eat
Hansel and Gretel.

The witch puts Hansel
into a cage.

The witch lights
a fire.

Is the fire hot?
says the witch
to Gretel.

It looks hot,
says Gretel.
Come and have a look.

The witch looks
into the fire.

In you go,
says Gretel.

Gretel says, Hansel!
The witch is in the fire!
We can go home.

Look, says Hansel.
Here is
some treasure.
We can have it.

They get the treasure,
and find the way home.

The stepmother
has gone.

The woodcutter says,
Stay here,
Hansel and Gretel.
It is good
to have you home.

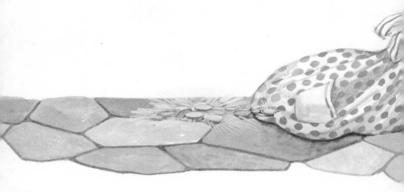